This book belongs to:

- - - - - - - - - - - -

to Piers —
the most hopeful gardener

Musgrove and

the Giant Turnip

by
Ilona Rodgers

Stacey International

It was Sunday afternoon. Musgrove was looking through his old newspapers. Hermione was sorting out the contents of the wooden glove box — foreign coins in one pile, odd buttons in another.

Presently she came across a crumpled envelope.

"What's this?" she asked Musgrove.

"Seeds," answered Musgrove – "seeds from Aunt Aurelia's prize-winning turnip. Don't you remember the photograph she sent us?"

"Of course I remember," said Hermione, and shook the tiny seeds into her hand. "What are you keeping them for?"

"I wanted to plant them," Musgrove sighed, "but we don't have a garden and I never found a suitable place in Notting Hill."

"What about Kensington Gardens?" suggested Hermione. "There are wild places there. Nobody will notice."

"Clever girl! Let's give it a try!" said Musgrove and up he got.

He put a watering can, a spade, a rake and Hermione into the dog cart and set off for Kensington Gardens.

After a long search Musgrove and Hermione found a secret place behind the statue of Peter Pan. They raked aside the dead leaves. Musgrove dug a hole.

Hermione put seeds into it and covered them with earth.

They fetched some water
from the Serpentine, watered
the ground and marked
the spot with three sticks.
　　Every day Musgrove and
Hermione came back and
sat there waiting.
　　Nothing happened.
"Maybe the seeds were too old,"
wondered Hermione, "or maybe
the woodlice ate them."

Then, one day, they saw
a green shoot with a thin,
pale stem and two round leaves.

It was very small.
Just like this.

Day by day it grew bigger...

and bigger...

and bigger.

Musgrove got worried. "Hermione," he said, "we'd better pull it out before somebody notices." He took hold of the leaves and pulled.

Nothing happened.

He pulled again.

Still nothing.

"I'll help you!" cried Hermione and pulled at Musgrove's coat as hard as she could.

"Gently!" Musgrove squealed. "That hurts."

"What's all this noise about?"
came a voice behind them.
It was Park Attendant Cluff,
who chanced to pass by.
"It's about pulling out a
turnip, Officer," explained Musgrove.
"Would you mind giving us a hand?"
"'Fraid I can't. Not insured for
pulling," apologized the Attendant.
"But I can build you a team.
Just spent the whole week on
a Team Building Course." And
before Musgrove could answer,

Park Attendant Cluff called to
the Old Lady who was feeding
an ice-cream to a stray dog,
and to Mr. Maggs the ice-cream

man with his cold cat:
  "You, gentle folk, come and
help this Rat in distress
to pull out his legume!"

Attendant Cluff climbed on to the statue of Peter Pan. Everybody gathered around.

"Men to pull! I to whistle! Women and children to cheer!" commanded Park Attendant Cluff. "Take your positions!"

"How do we cheer?" Hermione asked the Old Lady.

"I suppose the way they do at the Opera," the lady replied.

Officer Cluff drew a deep breath and with all his might blew the whistle.

Musgrove pulled the Turnip. Mr. Maggs pulled Musgrove. The Old Lady cried, "Encore!" Hermione cried, "Bravo!"

The stray dog dropped his ice-cream and barked.

The cold cat stole the ice-cream and ate it.

Only the Turnip did nothing.

"It would be easier to shift Peter Pan than this blessed mangel-wurzel," grumbled Cluff. "We are reduced to seeking help of women and children," he declared.

So the Old Lady lined up behind
Mr. Maggs, Hermione behind the
Old Lady. They all pulled.
The Turnip didn't budge an inch.

"Animals to the rescue!" cried Cluff in desperation, and blew his whistle again.

Musgrove pulled the Turnip.

Mr. Maggs pulled Musgrove.

The Old Lady pulled Mr. Maggs.
Hermione pulled the Old Lady.
The stray dog pulled Hermione.
The cold cat pulled the stray dog.
They pulled and pulled and ...

just at that moment a short-sighted duck from the Serpentine saw the cat's tail, mistook it for a hairy caterpillar and pulled it. And with the duck's pull the Turnip suddenly came out.

Everybody stared at it in silence. It was e-e-e-normous! The Old Lady spoke first. "Isn't it georgeous! Absolutely georgeous!" she called to

a photographer who was taking
pictures of the new plastic litter bins.
He took a picture of the Turnip
and gave it to the Kensington and
Notting Hill Globe, which everyone
reads, even Aunt Aurelia.

P. S. There are many more stories about Musgrove available from all good booksellers.

Stacey International
128 Kensington Church Street, London W8 4BH
Tel: +44 (0)207 221 7166   Fax: +44 (0)207 792 9288
E-mail: enquiries@stacey-international.co.uk
Website: www.stacey-international.co.uk

ISBN: 9781905299966

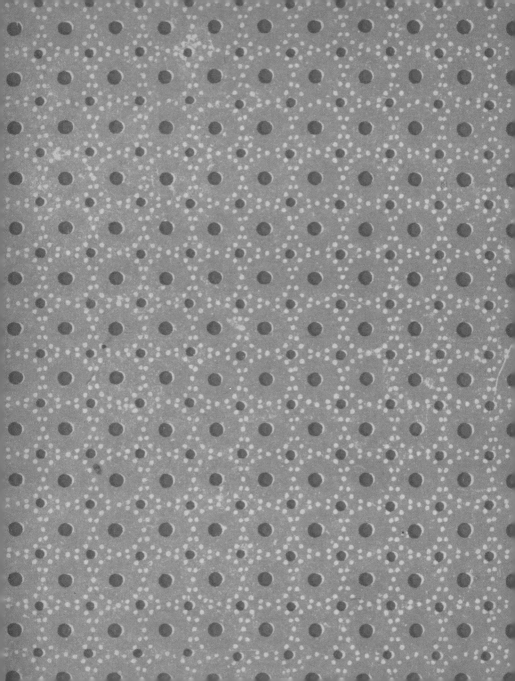